Francisco Menéndez

Although no portraits survive of Francisco Menendez, this is how one artist imagines he appeared, based on his heritage and the time period.

FORT Mose

AND THE STORY OF THE MAN WHO BUILT THE FIRST FREE BLACK SETTLEMENT IN COLONIAL AMERICA

Glennette Tilley Turner

Abrams Books for Young Readers ✷ New York

This book is dedicated to Darwin McBeth Walton, my friend and colleague,
and my 102-year-old neighbor, Mrs. L. C. Cash.

—G. T. T.

❖

A NOTE TO THE READER:

- The pattern used in the background and borders of this book is a combination of stylized tropical leaves. Tropical trees, such as palms, are prevalent in and around the area of St. Augustine, Florida.

- Both the National Park Service and the Fort Mose Historical Society Web sites spell *Mose* without an acute accent on the *e*. We purposely adopted this version of the spelling.

- The original colony of Carolina was divided into the colonies of North and South Carolina in 1710. Accordingly, this book uses the name Carolina when referring to points in time before 1710, and the names of the individual colonies for points thereafter.

❖

Library of Congress Cataloging-in-Publication Data

Turner, Glennette Tilley.
Fort Mose : and the story of the man who built the first free black settlement in colonial America / Glennette Turner.
p. cm.
Includes bibliographical references and index.
ISBN 978-0-8109-4056-7
1. Fort Mose Site (Fla.)—Juvenile literature. 2. Menendez, Francisco, b. ca. 1700—Juvenile literature. 3. Saint Augustine (Fla.)—Militia—History—18th century—Juvenile literature. 4. African Americans—Florida—Saint Augustine—Biography—Juvenile literature. 5. African Americans—Florida—Saint Augustine—History—18th century—Juvenile literature. 6. Free African Americans—Florida—Saint Augustine—History—18th century—Juvenile literature. 7. Fugitive slaves—Florida—Saint Augustine—History—18th century—Juvenile literature. 8. Frontier and pioneer life—Florida—Saint Augustine—Juvenile literature. 9. Saint Augustine (Fla.)—History—18th century—Juvenile literature. 10. Florida—History—Spanish colony, 1565–1763—Juvenile literature. I. Title.
F319.F734T87 2010
975.9'18—dc22
2009052205

Text copyright © 2010 Glennette Tilley Turner
Please see page 41 for illustration credits
Book design by Maria T. Middleton

Printed and bound in China
10 9 8 7 6 5 4

Abrams Books for Young Readers are available at special discounts when purchased in quantity for premiums and promotions as well as fundraising or educational use. Special editions can also be created to specification. For details, contact specialmarkets@abramsbooks.com or the address below.

ABRAMS The Art of Books
195 Broadway, New York, NY 10007
abramsbooks.com

CONTENTS

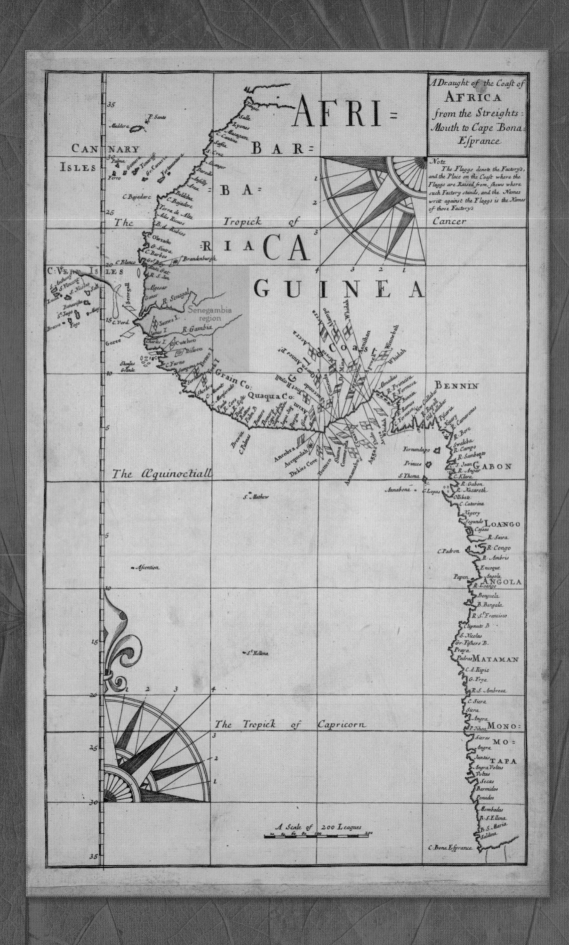

THE STORY OF FRANCISCO MENENDEZ

This remarkable story unfolded years before the battles of the Revolutionary War, the writing of the Declaration of Independence, and the signing of the United States Constitution. For Francisco Menendez, the story started in the Senegambia region of West Africa, where he was born into the Mandingo tribe around 1700.

There are no written records of the exact year of his birth, or of his birth name. He had several names during his life, ranging from those rooted in Mandingo tradition, to the name assigned to him by an English slaveholder in the South Carolina colony, and, finally, to the name he adopted prior to becoming captain of the black militia at Fort Mose (pronounced Mo-*say*) in Spanish Florida.

HIS EARLY LIFE IN AFRICA

The naming of a child was very meaningful and complex in Mandingo society. A name told many important things about who the person was. When the man who eventually became known as Francisco Menendez was born, his mother gave him his first, or individual, name. That name indicated his birth order: whether he was his mother's first, second, third, or fourth son. However, this name was just temporary. A few days later, his father or another influential man in the village presided over a ceremony during which the baby boy's head was shaved. The person conducting the ceremony then gave the baby a permanent—or true—name. The baby would have also had a clan name that linked him to the ancient founder of his extended family.

If the baby who became Francisco Menendez had grown up in his village, he would have kept his permanent name for the rest of his life. Perhaps he would have added a title to that name if he had accomplished some outstanding deed.

During his childhood, Francisco Menendez would have taken instruction from wise, influential men in the Muslim religion known as marabouts (pronounced "marabu"). An important part of his education would have been learning about the rich heritage of the Mandingo people. One of the first lessons a marabout would teach was that the ancestors of the Mandingo had come from Manding, the ancient Mali empire. The history of Mali has been traced back to prehistoric times through rock paintings and carvings. At its height this major African civilization occupied much of the northern half of West Africa. The Mali empire was in

a strategic trading position, and its great camel caravans conducted trade across the Sahara Desert. Its greatest leader, Mansa Musa, was widely recognized for his sense of fairness and ability to govern. Even traders and merchants from other countries had the highest respect for him. This is what Ibn Batuta, a North African scholar and traveler who visited Mali in the early fourteenth century, observed:

The state of affairs among these people is indeed extraordinary. . . . They are seldom unjust, and have a greater abhorrence of injustice than any other people. . . . There is complete security in their country. Neither traveler nor inhabitant in it has anything to fear from robbers or men of violence.

Hearing stories about the Mali kingdom and its great leaders would have intrigued any young man. Perhaps they inspired Francisco Menendez to become a leader himself.

From early childhood, Menendez, like all other boys in Mandingo society, would have looked forward to the Rite of Passage, which prepared boys between the ages of six and thirteen for manhood. During this secret ritual, young men, known as novices, were circumcised and taught the values of the society and such survival skills as how to identify and use healing plants. From that time onward they began to relate to their family members as adults rather than as children.

The life lessons Francisco Menendez learned during his formative years later helped him cope with circumstances he could never have imagined. No records show how long it was after the Rite of Passage that Menendez was captured by slavers. Perhaps he had been out building dikes for the rice fields, piloting a boat on the Gambia River, or going on a mission for his village.

Once enslaved, he would have been shackled to other people who had also been captured as they were living their daily lives. Most likely Francisco Menendez and his fellow captives traveled toward the village of Juffure on the Gambia River. They would have been forced to march for days, weeks, or longer in the blistering sun. If captives got tired or had an itch, they were not allowed to stop and rest or scratch. Many captives did not survive such a journey. Bleached bones of people who had died were scattered along the trail.

When the survivors reached Juffure, they were put on public display. They were stripped and their bodies closely examined. The new slaves were traded for such goods as iron bars and guns.

Then they were taken to James Island, which was the site of one of the English "slave castles" on the west coast of Africa. Inside the castles they were crowded into dark, stone dungeons. There they were held until slave ships arrived, and they often lost their will to live.

Francisco Menendez must have thought of his family and his village. Would he ever be able to return home? What would happen next? He could never have imagined the horrors that awaited him. He would need to be strong physically, mentally, and spiritually to survive.

When a slave ship arrived, Francisco Menendez and his fellow captives would have been herded through a one-way door from the slave castle onto the ship. The enslaved were chained together shoulder to shoulder and then bolted to the floor of a lower deck. One captive later described the experience this way:

The filth, the stench, the loss of life, the disease, the packing of men in spaces so tight they could neither turn, nor stand, nor squat, nor sit, is beyond human comprehension. Yet such were the conditions that . . . people were forced to bear during the hellish journey from Africa to the New World—the journey known as the Middle Passage or Maafa ("the massive disaster").

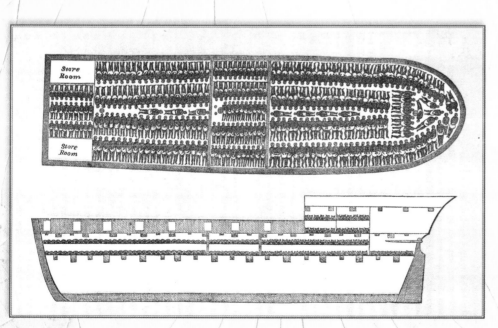

OPPOSITE PAGE, TOP: *Slavers prepare to carry off captured Africans.*

OPPOSITE PAGE, CENTER: *Ruins of the village of Juffure, where Menendez may have been held in captivity.*

OPPOSITE PAGE, BOTTOM: *A drawing of James Island and its "slave castle."*

LEFT: *A depiction of how slaves were chained together in the lower deck of a ship.*

A view of Charles Town harbor in 1760. The town was renamed Charleston in 1783.

If the seas were calm, the ship would have reached the English port of Charles Town, South Carolina, in a month or so. In stormy weather the voyage across the Atlantic Ocean would have taken five to twelve weeks. Upon reaching port, Francisco Menendez and his fellow captives who had survived the Middle Passage were taken to Sullivan's Island, off the coast of Charles Town. They were held in a pestilence, or "pest," house, quarantined in case they were carriers of contagious diseases. It was here that the captured were subjected to a process called "seasoning," which was intended to prepare them to be docile and willingly accept servitude. They were often beaten and nearly starved in the attempt to destroy their will to fight or escape.

After ten days on Sullivan's Island, Francisco Menendez and the other Africans were sold at auction on the streets of Charles Town. They were given close physical inspection and purchased by slaveholders to do every kind of work that was needed for the operation of a plantation, from digging up tree roots to prepare the forest land for farming, to cooking, cleaning, and taking care of large households.

Just as Francisco Menendez's Mandingo name is unknown, so is the English name that was assigned to him by the South Carolina slaveholder who purchased him. Because of this, it is not possible to know exactly when he arrived in Charles Town, or to identify what ship he arrived on or which slaveholder bought him.

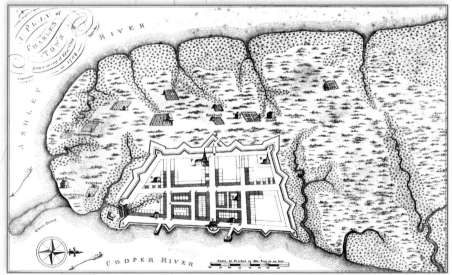

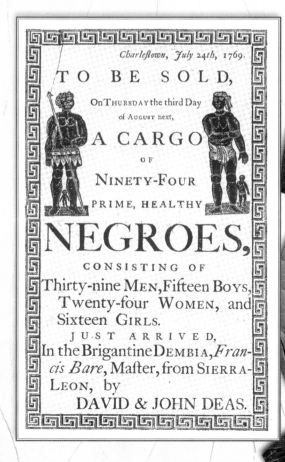

ABOVE: *A map of Charles Town, 1704.*

ABOVE, RIGHT: *A slave auction in New York City as imagined by Howard Pyle. Slave auctions in the Carolinas would have been similar.*

RIGHT: *A poster for a slave auction, 1769.*

The Origins of Charleston and of Rice as an Export Crop

IN 1670, EIGHT MEN FROM BARBADOS who were loyal supporters of English king Charles II established a small settlement on the west bank of the Ashley River in the Carolina colony. (The colony of Carolina was separated in 1710 into North and South Carolina.) They named the town Charles Town in honor of the king. The men who established Charles Town, Carolina, were known as the Lords Proprietors. The Proprietors began a search that was continued by planters who came after to find a product that would bring them great profits. At first they experimented with growing cotton, olives, ginger, tobacco, and grapes. They also tried raising cattle. They found that they could sell animal furs and pelts at a profit, but they had a strained relationship with the Native peoples who lived in the area and who did much of the fur trapping.

Through trial and error, the Proprietors and other settlers found that rice had the potential to be the most profitable crop. They saw its value as an export item. There was a strain of rice actually called Carolina Gold, and it brought great wealth. However, it required a very specialized type of cultivation. The marshlands, waters, and high temperatures made the Low Country (the coastal counties of South Carolina, including the Sea Islands) ideal for growing rice.

South Carolina planters soon realized the advantage of importing slaves from the "Rice Coast" of West Africa, which included what were then called Senegambia, Sierra Leone, and the Windward Coast. They paid the highest prices for slaves from this region because, over the centuries, Africans from there had developed specialized labor patterns and technical knowledge for rice cultivation. As a result, Africans were imported in ever-increasing numbers. Prior to 1710, slave imports rarely exceeded three hundred a year. By the 1720s, they numbered two thousand annually.

In addition to being experienced in rice cultivation, the Africans were able to adjust to the semitropical climate in the Low Country, since it was similar to that of their homelands. Having lived in that type of climate, they had built up immunity to such tropical diseases as malaria.

This was not the case with the European colonists. As a result, most plantation owners lived in Charles Town, which had drier, less humid weather conditions, and they left overseers in charge of the large, rice-producing coastal plantations.

LIFE IN ENGLAND'S AMERICA

It is not known where in South Carolina Francisco Menendez was held in bondage or what kind of work he was required to perform. Strength and skill counted for more than age in determining what tasks slaves were given. To judge from the personal qualities he demonstrated later in his life, he was highly intelligent, was able to make the most of opportunities, and possessed leadership ability.

If he was enslaved in Charles Town, he could have been given any of a number of tasks. The possibilities include being a gentleman's servant or coachman, performing general household duties, working on the docks, or being hired out to a shopkeeper. He may have encountered merchants, Indian traders, fishermen, smugglers, and sailors who sailed in and out of this major seaport.

Perhaps Francisco Menendez proved himself to be so capable at the tasks he was given that he was presented with opportunities to further develop his abilities. Whatever his tasks were, they probably did not require knowledge of the three Rs, because slaveholders went to great lengths to prevent enslaved people from learning to read and write.

Although Menendez knew how to read and write Arabic and was able to speak several African languages before being enslaved, he may well have kept this knowledge a secret. Many slaveholders believed that literacy made slaves less malleable and dependent, and that it empowered them to gain information and to forge documents that could enable them to escape.

The Old Plantation, *1790. Here, Gullah slaves dance and play musical instruments derived from African instruments, such as the* shegureh, *a rattle. The free people of Fort Mose also incorporated instruments and tools from Africa into their daily lives.*

If Francisco Menendez was enslaved in the Low Country, he would have had a sense of community. Living among fellow Africans, including others from the Mandingo tribe, Menendez would have found people who had religious beliefs and cultural traditions that were similar to those he had known as a young child. Music and storytelling would have brought back fond memories. Since not all of the enslaved Africans spoke the same language, they developed a way to communicate, in what became known as the Gullah language, which blended the languages spoken by the Africans, the English, and the Indians.

In the Low Country, Menendez may have trapped animals, hunted, or herded cattle. It is likely that he performed tasks related to rice cultivation, such as clearing fields, harvesting, hollowing out tree trunks to function as water pipes, building dikes for the rice fields, or digging ditches or canals.

There were numerous creeks, rivers, and streams throughout the Low Country. Because of the difficulties of overland travel, it was these waterways that linked the area to the world beyond the South

Carolina coast. Like many Africans who had lived along the water before being captured, Menendez may have had experience piloting boats and fishing in his homeland. Because these skills were highly valued by plantation owners, he may have had a chance to use this knowledge to transport people and goods or to work as a fisherman.

Or Menendez may have relied on his ability to speak more than one language. Each year thousands of deerskins and other pelts were exported from South Carolina to England. According to historian Peter H. Wood, "while most of the hunting and trapping was done by Indians and the procurement and export managed by whites," enslaved Africans were active in most intermediate stages of the trade. They often served as interpreters during trade transactions and "were among those who regularly rowed up the Savannah River . . . and returned downstream with boatloads of skins."

Such tasks may have given Francisco Menendez the mobility to learn of news beyond the plantation and to interact with the Yamasee Indians.

Through one means or another, he had an opportunity to come in contact with the Yamasee and learn two life-changing pieces of information. Menendez discovered that they did not like the English and that the Spanish in Florida would *grant freedom* to enslaved Africans who could reach the town of St. Augustine.

Native Americans had inhabited all of South Carolina prior to the arrival of the colonists. The tribes included the Kiawah, the Edisto, the Etiwan, the Kusso, the Sewee, the Catawba, the Cherokee, the Creek, and the Yamasee. Losing much of their land to, and being enslaved by, the newcomers created ongoing tension between the Indians and the English. So did the fact that the colonists created rivalries among the Native nations by providing firearms to some and not to others.

To some extent, the Indians coexisted with the English. They conducted a lucrative trade in deerskins and fur pelts with the settlers, served as guides through the southern wilderness, and sometimes recaptured Africans who had escaped from bondage.

For the most part, though, Africans and Indians recognized that they had many things in common and that a relationship could be of mutual benefit. Both peoples had comparable experiences living in subtropical coastal lands. Both knew the survival skills of trapping, hunting, and foraging for edible and medicinal plants. Both were keen observers of the natural world. Both had mastered many guerrilla fighting techniques.

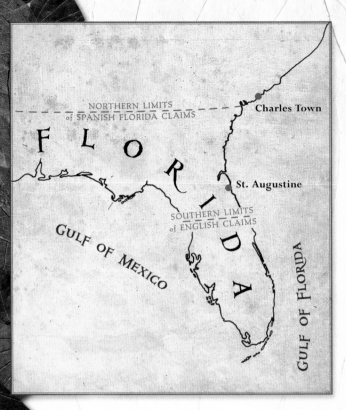

A map depicting the English and Spanish Florida claims.

Far more Indians remained free than were enslaved. Many lived in areas that bordered the rice plantations, and they often provided sanctuary or safe passage to enslaved Indians or Africans who escaped. Many had not had as much direct contact with the English as the Africans had. As a result they welcomed Africans who had learned to speak and understand the English language and who could serve as interpreters in dealings with the English.

But perhaps the greatest thing they had in common was that Africans and Indians had both been subjugated by the English. Both had known freedom, and they yearned to experience it again.

Through his interaction with the Yamasee, Francisco Menendez learned to speak their language. He also learned of a decisive action they planned to take: They were going to wage war. The Yamasee intended to push the colonists out of their homeland. After living for decades at the mercy of the English, in 1715 they formed an alliance of almost all the Native nations between St. Augustine and Cape Fear to fight in the Yamasee War.

Somehow Francisco Menendez escaped his English owners and fought in the Yamasee War alongside the Native people for three years. Language ability was not the only skill he had to offer. Like many other enslaved Africans, he probably had some training in warfare during the years in his homeland. Unlike him, large numbers of Africans could not choose which side of the war to fight on.

The colonists had long been aware that there were Africans with military experience among their enslaved labor force. They considered this to be simultaneously a potential source of danger and an asset. Prior to the Yamasee War, they had armed enslaved Africans in an effort to bolster the colonial forces.

Africans helped fight every military threat to the colonies. The importance of the enslaved Africans was demonstrated by the fact that slaveholders could be fined in times of alarm for failing to muster out each slave on the militia rolls. During the Yamasee War, the colonists equipped them with guns and lances and pressed them into military service by the hundreds. According to Peter H. Wood:

In simple proportional terms Negroes may never have played such a major role in any earlier or later American conflict as they did in the Yamasee War of 1715. The history of this . . . struggle, which was so vital to the interests of red, white, and black in the Southeast, has never been adequately pieced together.

The war posed a highly serious threat to the colonists. A firsthand report written by the Reverend Le Jau relates that the outlook was "dismal in all respects. The Province is in danger of being Lost & our Lives are Threatened."

The value of the contribution by African fighters in the ensuing campaign was evident in a journal written by an officer in the South Carolina forces. He stated, "Their importance was increased by the absence of significant aid from Virginia." That summer many fighters on both sides were killed as the Native forces attacked the colonists' settlements. The outcome of the war was uncertain.

Not all South Carolinians supported the colonists' views. A small number of English speakers thought the war was a kind of justice visited upon the whites. The vicar of the Anglican congregation in Charles Town wrote, "[A]ll we can doe is, to lament in Secret those Sins, which have brought this Judgement upon us."

The alliance of Native nations almost succeeded in exterminating the English in the area. However, with the eventual help of reinforcements from Virginia and North Carolina and the assistance of loyal Indians, the colonial forces were able to overpower the Yamasee and their allies and force them to scatter to locations far from their homelands.

The Creek migrated in the direction of Louisiana. Other Native nations were decimated and dispersed. Some Edisto and Etiwan, whose livelihood depended on the deerskin trade with the English, remained in the Charles Town area. After making their way through the almost three hundred miles of swamps and dense forests, navigating alligator-infested rivers, withstanding Atlantic hurricanes, and eluding English slave catchers, the Yamasee and their African contingent, including Francisco Menendez, eventually reached Spanish Florida.

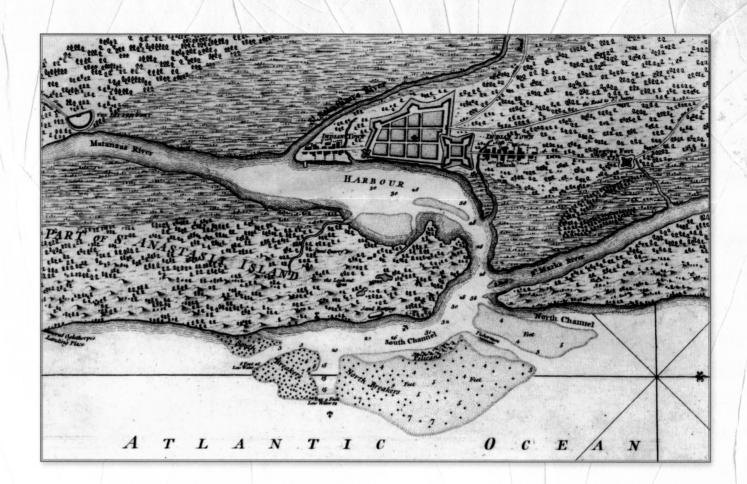

ABOVE: *A map of the town and harbor of St. Augustine, 1762.*

OPPOSITE PAGE: *St. Augustine in 1673. The city was known as a haven for fugitive slaves.*

LIFE IN SPAIN'S AMERICA

In 1724, Francisco Menendez and nine other African men arrived in St. Augustine, with the help of English-speaking Yamasee Indians. The Africans had heard rumors that many years earlier King Charles II of Spain had issued a royal edict giving "liberty to all . . . the men as well as the women . . ." Because of this, Menendez and the other men expected to become freemen as soon as they sought baptism and converted to Catholicism.

Somehow, at some point following the Yamasee War, a Yamasee known as Mad Dog gained control of Francisco Menendez's fate and sold him to the Spanish after he reached Florida. Details of the timing and circumstances of that sale are unknown.

At first the Spanish governor, Antonio de Benavides, seemed to honor the edict to free the slaves. He sent a delegation to Charles Town to negotiate an agreement on the runaways and offered to purchase them for two hundred pesos each. He also wrote to the authorities in Spain, but he had not received a reply when the English made threats to come and reclaim Menendez and the other Africans who arrived with him. Governor Benavides's response was to sell the men locally. He justified his action by arguing that he feared the English might come to reclaim them by force. He then used money from the sale to reimburse the English slaveholders who complained about the loss of their "property."

Francisco Menendez and the nine other men were purchased by some of the most prominent citizens of St. Augustine. Menendez was purchased by the royal accountant Don Francisco Menendez. Some of the other nine were purchased by the royal treasurer, military officers, and even some religious officials. Others were sold to owners who took them to Havana, Cuba.

The Land Disputes of Florida

King Charles II of Spain (1661–1700).

THERE HAD BEEN AN ONGOING struggle between Spanish and English forces for control of the area between Charles Town and St. Augustine since the English established Charles Town in 1670. Military skirmishes and encounters escalated through the next century.

In 1686, Spanish forces, which included Africans and Indians, raided two English settlements along the Carolina coast. They captured thirteen Africans in those raids. The following year, a group of eight African men, two women, and a small child reached St. Augustine in a canoe, and the Spanish gave them sanctuary. The Spanish refused to return them to Carolina after they converted to Catholicism.

Six years later, in 1693, Spanish king Charles II issued his decree granting freedom to any slave who escaped to Florida and became Catholic. English slaveholders were outraged.

During sieges led by Carolina governor James Moore in 1702 and 1704, the town of St. Augustine and most Spanish frontier missions were burned down. St. Augustine was rebuilt, but Spanish activity in east Florida was limited to this town.

Large numbers of enslaved Africans continued to seek refuge there. They set out for the unknown, venturing through dangerous swamps and battling slave catchers in the attempt to reach St. Augustine.

Although re-enslaved, Francisco Menendez was appointed by Governor Antonio de Benavides to command a black militia. Menendez and his men helped defend St. Augustine against an attack of the South Carolina militia led by Colonel John Palmer in 1728.

In 1733, Spanish king Philip V issued two new edicts. According to the first of these edicts, there would be no future reimbursement made to the English for the loss of their slaves. It also restated the offer of freedom. The second edict commended Menendez's men for their bravery, but it indicated that they would be required to complete four years of royal service before they would be freed.

Although he was enslaved by the royal accountant, Don Francisco Menendez, and yearned to be fully free, Francisco Menendez and the accountant apparently had high regard for each other. When it came time to select a Spanish name for himself, Francisco Menendez adopted the very same name as that of the accountant. While working for such a high Spanish official, he may have learned a lot about government. During his period of servitude, Menendez applied his talent for learning languages to learning to read and write Spanish.

He put his newly acquired knowledge to good use. Ever mindful that he and the men he had escaped with had come to St. Augustine seeking complete freedom, he petitioned Governor Benavides and the auxiliary bishop of Cuba. Nothing came of Menendez's request.

Black militias were important in the defense of the Spanish colonies. TOP: *A seventeenth-century image of a Puerto Rican soldier.* BOTTOM: *A late-eighteenth-century image of a Panamanian artilleryman. Menendez and his militia would have dressed in a similar fashion.*

In 1737, Manuel de Montiano became the new governor of Florida, and once again Francisco Menendez petitioned for freedom. This time a Yamasee cacique, or chief, named Jorge supported his petition. Chief Jorge stated that Captain Menendez and three other Africans had fought bravely for three years during the Yamasee War. Although Menendez and the others had been patient and "more than loyal," they had been betrayed by a "heathen" named Mad Dog. However, Chief Jorge did not blame Mad Dog. Instead, he blamed the Spanish who had purchased these loyal allies.

After reviewing the case, the new governor granted unconditional freedom to the petitioners on March 15, 1738. Following this, Governor Montiano established the freemen from South Carolina in a new town under the leadership of Captain Menendez. The new town, Gracia Real de Santa Teresa de Mose (Fort Mose), became the first officially sanctioned free black town in what is now the United States.

The Franciscan priests of St. Augustine would have dressed in a style similar to this Franciscan priest, who lived in California in the early eighteenth century.

THE BUILDING OF FORT MOSE

The name of the town combined an existing Indian place-name, Mose, with the phrase *Gracia Real*, which indicated that it was established by the king, and the name of the town's patron saint, Teresa of Avilés. By the time Fort Mose was established, approximately one hundred formerly enslaved Africans were living in St. Augustine. Most of them had been born free in West Africa before being captured and transported to America. Fort Mose was the early, southern destination of the resistance movement that would later become known as the Underground Railroad.

Following colonial tradition, the Spanish governor assigned a white military officer and royal official to supervise the new community. The governor also posted a student priest to instruct the residents in church doctrine and "good customs." The priest lived at Mose, but there are no documents that show that the Spanish officers did.

LEFT: *A drawing of a Spanish mission similar to the one that would have been constructed at Fort Mose. The buildings were made of wooden boards with thatched palm roofs.*

BOTTOM, LEFT AND RIGHT: *Sketches of two forts, Picalata (now commonly spelled "Picolata") and Pupo, constructed in a style similar to that of Fort Mose.*

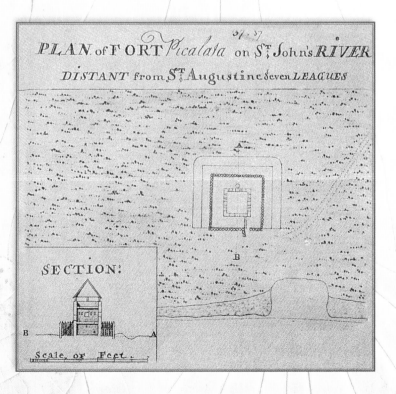

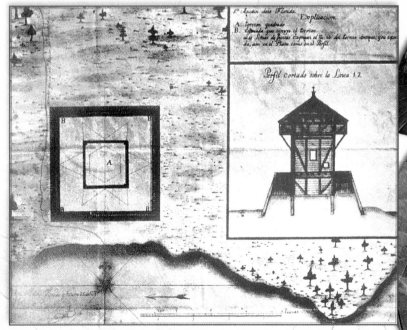

To the Spanish, the fort was a first line of defense against any future English attacks. To the newly freed inhabitants of the town, it was liberty at last!

For the first time since they were enslaved by the English, African men and women could legally marry, have the right to own property, feel secure that their family members would not be sold, be paid for their labor, and make legal contracts.

The recently freed militiamen and their families moved to the new frontier. There they built a "fortress of freedom." It was a walled fort that, according to English sources, was constructed of stone, "four square with a flanker at each corner, banked with earth, having a ditch without on all sides lined round with prickly royal [cactus] and [having] a well and house within, and a lookout."

Spanish reports described the town site as being surrounded by fertile lands and nearby forests, and having a river of salt water "running through it." The townspeople soon planted fields, cut trees they needed for building materials, and caught fish and shellfish to supplement their diet.

Most residents of Mose lived in small, often oval-shaped, palm-thatched huts outside the fort. These huts, known as *chosa*, were described as "resembling thatched Indian huts" and may have been much like the dwellings the Africans had in their homelands.

Residents of Fort Mose were very aware that their being there was as important to the Spanish as it was to them. Their fortress was strategically significant, for it was the northern outpost situated at the head of Mose Creek, with access to St. Augustine about two miles to the south. It was also at the crossroads of two major overland trails: the northbound San Nicholas trail and the westbound Apalache trail.

They were also aware that they lived under the ever-present danger of attack. Even so, if it was the price of freedom, the residents of Mose were willing to pay it. Members of the Mose militia would rather die than let themselves be taken back into slavery. They vowed to be "the most cruel enemies of the English" and to spill "their last drop of blood in defense of the Great crown of Spain and the Holy Faith."

News of Fort Mose quickly spread to the South Carolina slaveholders and some of the Africans on the rice plantations—and to the new English colony of Georgia. The South Carolina planters had strong objections to Spain's sanctuary policy and to the very existence of Fort Mose. They took increasingly desperate measures to contain their enslaved laborers, but to no avail. Enslaved Africans responded to the news by escaping south in ever-increasing numbers.

In 1738 there were thirty-eight households of men, women, and children at Fort Mose.

OPPOSITE PAGE: *These thatched-roof huts in West Africa, photographed in 1973, are similar to those constructed hundreds of years ago. Menendez would have been familiar with their design.*

ABOVE: *A Florida Timucua Indian village of the late sixteenth century. This image and the one opposite illustrate the influences of West African and Native American dwellings on the Spanish communities of colonial Florida (see top image page 19), especially the thatched roofs.*

Of course, one of the men was Francisco Menendez. He married Ana Maria de Escovar, who, like her husband, was Mandingo. Research has not yet revealed how or when they met or when she arrived at Fort Mose. And questions remain about the exact composition of their family.

Living at Fort Mose was not an easy existence. Its residents had constant concerns about food and defense, not only from the English colonists but also from some unfriendly Indians who lived in the area. Francisco Menendez knew that even with skilled workers and fertile lands, it would take time to produce enough food to feed Fort Mose's citizens, become self-sustaining, and eventually produce a surplus to supply the residents of St. Augustine.

The Catholic Spanish government considered the Fort Mose residents a community of religious converts. Just as it did for other such emerging communities, it provided biscuits, corn, beef, and other provisions from government stores to help the residents.

Francisco Menendez had to have been pleased that life at Fort Mose settled into a daily routine. In addition to the trades they had been taught on the plantations where they had worked, many residents remembered traditions and technologies they had brought from Africa that made them more efficient in their work. Blacksmiths, farmers, lumberjacks, sawyers, carpenters, boatmen, fishermen, homemakers, and soldiers all offered their services. Cowboys rounded up wild horses and cattle. Some residents traveled the two miles into St. Augustine to work and to trade. Others remained at the fort, performing tasks that were needed there.

African culture influenced aspects of everyday life in Mose, ranging from crafts, dress, and religious practices to methods of farming. For most, this was the first time since being enslaved that they could freely express themselves through their traditional songs and dances. Like the Spaniards, Mose residents adopted many local Indian traditions, particularly the extensive use of Indian pottery for cooking and food storage.

Fort Mose provided a safe haven for people who had been born in Mandingo, Carabali, Congo, and other West African culture areas, and for Native people who had lived along the Atlantic seacoast before the arrival of the Europeans. All of these groups had made perilous journeys from the Carolinas and Virginia, as well as from Cuba, Barbados, and elsewhere in the Caribbean. Many had reached their destination on foot or by canoe.

In their leisure hours, parents surely told their children stories they had heard in Africa or on the plantations, about how Brer Rabbit or another creature used its wits to outsmart a stronger, more powerful animal. The stories must have had new meaning to people who had outwitted slave catchers to reach Florida. The residents of Mose enjoyed close family ties. Africans, Indians, and Spaniards lived and worked in harmony.

OPPOSITE PAGE: *These two images show the influence of European dress and African musical instruments on Spanish American culture.*

ABOVE, LEFT: *African blacksmiths were able to adopt their skills easily to the needs of colonial America, both as slaves and as freemen.*

ABOVE, RIGHT: *An illustration of Brer Rabbit published in 1892 in the book* Uncle Remus and His Friends, *by Joel Chandler Harris.*

News of the freedom enjoyed by residents of Fort Mose continued to reach people still enslaved on Carolina plantations. It was spread by word of mouth on the slave grapevine. Coachmen and others who had a chance to travel away from their plantations and come in contact with other Africans and Indians shared whatever information they learned. Many people dreamed of escaping to Mose. And many tried.

SLAVE REVOLTS AND THEIR EFFECT

Early on Sunday, September 9, 1739, an Angolan slave by the name of Jemmy led about twenty African men to a bridge on the Stono River near Charles Town. The men broke into a gun store and some houses and killed the shopkeepers and the occupants of the homes. They spared an innkeeper, "for he was a good man and kind to his slaves."

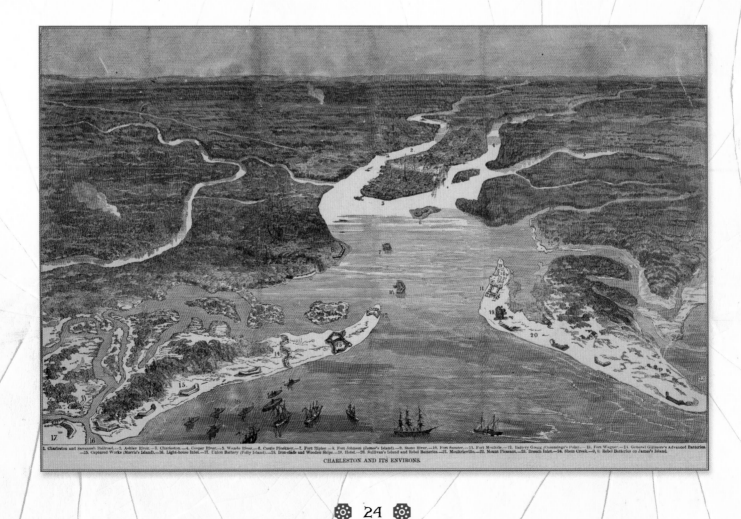

1. Charleston and Savannah Railroad.—2. Ashley River.—3. Charleston.—4. Cooper River.—5. Wando River.—6. Castle Pinckney.—7. Fort Ripley.—8. Fort Johnson (James's Island).—9. Stono River.—10. Fort Sumter.—11. Fort Moultrie.—12. Battery Gregg (Cumming's Point).—13. Fort Wagner.—14. General Gilmore's Advanced Batteries.—15. Captured Works (Morris's Island).—16. Light-house Inlet.—17. Union Battery (Folly Island).—18. Iron-clads and Wooden Ships.—19. Hotel.—20. Sullivan's Island and Rebel Batteries.—21. Moultrieville.—22. Mount Pleasant.—23. Breach Inlet.—24. Shem Creek.—G. G. Rebel Batteries on James's Island.

CHARLESTON AND ITS ENVIRONS.

HORRID MASSACRE IN VIRGINIA.

Other men joined Jemmy's fighters. They raised a banner that made them feel invincible. They shouted, "Liberty!" as they marched toward St. Augustine. They stopped in an open field and beat their drums and danced in preparation for battle and attempted to attract more enslaved Africans to join them. This gave slaveholders a chance to sound the alarm and surround them. About equal numbers of slaveholders and Africans were killed in the pitched battle that followed. About sixty Africans escaped. By the following Saturday, they had traveled thirty miles closer to St. Augustine when the slaveholders, aided by reinforcements, caught up with and defeated them. Accounts of the rebellion reported that some of Jemmy's men escaped. It is not known if any succeeded in reaching Fort Mose.

The Stono Rebellion had come very close to succeeding. The slaveholders hurriedly passed stringent new laws in an attempt to prevent future slave revolts. These laws prohibited slaves from growing their own food, assembling in groups, earning money, or learning to read. It also barred slaveholders from freeing slaves.

The bitter feelings between the Spanish and the English colonists in South Carolina and Georgia worsened. The Spanish viewed Georgia as an illegal colony that encroached on their territory.

General James Oglethorpe.

Two related events took place in 1740. In June, approximately 150 slaves rebelled on the Ashley River outside of Charles Town. They may also have been trying to reach Mose. South Carolina's stringent new laws were enforced, and fifty of the rebels were captured and hanged. Some of the remaining hundred may have made their way to Mose.

At the same time, the English general James Oglethorpe led a major expeditionary force—made up of regiments of South Carolina and Georgia, a huge army of Indian allies, and seven warships—against St. Augustine and Fort Mose.

Governor Montiano relied heavily on Francisco Menendez's militia. Menendez led guerrilla units composed of equal numbers of experienced and well-trained free Africans, Indians, and Spaniards. They patrolled the frontier, collected valuable military intelligence, and helped to fortify the provincial defenses.

Indian allies of the English and other troops fighting for General Oglethorpe also roamed the frontier. General Oglethorpe captured two Spanish forts west of St. Augustine and then headed for Fort Mose, where his lieutenants seized two Mose residents.

Realizing that he would be unable to protect Fort Mose, Governor Montiano ordered all its residents and two thousand residents of St. Augustine to take shelter in the Castillo de San Marcos, the much larger, main fortress built to protect St. Augustine. Rations were in short supply, and Governor Montiano pleaded with Cuba to send reinforcements and food.

The British occupied the abandoned Fort Mose. They dismantled the gate and damaged the walls. Meanwhile, General Oglethorpe's warships assaulted St. Augustine daily for almost a month.

Before daybreak on June 14, 1740, Captain Francisco Menendez, along with the Spanish forces, launched a surprise attack on Fort Mose. Engaging in hand-to-hand combat, they overtook the unsuspecting invaders and recaptured their fort. This battle was the turning point of the conflict.

It devastated General Oglethorpe's combined British forces. They referred to it as "Fatal Mose." Colonel John Palmer, who had led the British invasion of St. Augustine, was mortally wounded during the battle. General Oglethorpe soon withdrew. In the meantime, Cuban reinforcements came to the aid of the Spanish.

PETITIONS TO THE KING

Governor Montiano was so impressed with the performance of Captain Menendez's fighters, as well as that of the Spanish militia, that he wrote the king of Spain to commend the troops. He went beyond this and wrote a special recommendation praising Francisco Menendez for his extraordinary valor in battle and bravery during dangerous reconnaissance missions. He stated that Menendez had

distinguished himself in the establishment and cultivation of Mose, to improve the settlement, doing all he could so that the rest of his subjects, following his example, would apply themselves to work and learn good customs.

While the governor's praise was quite a compliment, it did not provide the reward Menendez felt he had earned. So he petitioned the king in an effort to receive a salary. He wrote, requesting a fair reward for

loyalty, zeal, and love I have always demonstrated in the royal service, in the encounters with the enemies, as well as in the effort and care with which I have worked to repair two bastions on the defense line of this plaza, being pleased to do it, although it advanced my poverty, and I have continually been in arms, and assisted in the maintenance of the bastions, without the least royal expense, despite the scarcity in which this presidio always exists, especially on this occasion.

Receiving no response, he filed a second petition several months later. He wrote both of his petitions in Spanish and signed his name with a flourish.

After a year of waiting for a response, Menendez decided on another plan. He would go to sea as a corsair, or pirate. His would sail first to Havana, Cuba, and from there to Spain. Menendez hoped that once he reached Spain, he would be able to get an audience with King Philip V and convince the monarch to reward him for his services. He began his journey by boarding a corsair ship in St. Augustine and taking a commission as a privateer.

An example of a privateer ship, similar to what Menendez may have sailed.

Piracy on the high seas was an accepted practice during this time. The prizes captured by British and Spanish privateer ships brought badly needed funds to their respective governments. St. Augustine had not received government subsidies for a number of years and encouraged piracy. These ships were manned by volunteers, some from the free black community. Although Spain welcomed their service, if they were captured, the British assumed they were slaves and sold them.

In July 1741, Menendez was captured by the British ship *Revenge*. When his captors realized that he was in fact the captain of the company that retook Mose from General Oglethorpe, they took revenge. They tied him to a gun, gave him two hundred lashes, "pickled him" in brine (salt water), and threatened even more serious bodily harm.

When the *Revenge* landed in the Bahamas, its commander, Benjamin Norton, stood to make a large profit. He argued in Admiralty Court that Menendez should be sold as a prize of war. The court agreed, and Menendez was sold into slavery once again. What happened to him between the years of 1741 and 1751 is a mystery, but somehow by 1752 he was back in charge of Fort Mose.

Rebuilding Fort Mose

Meanwhile, the former residents of Mose were still living in St. Augustine. Like other residents of that town, they were facing hard times. Three years before Menendez returned, Melchor de Navarrete had succeeded Manuel de Montiano as the governor of Florida. The new governor decided to reestablish Fort Mose, and he resettled the fort in a slightly different location on Mose Creek. The new fort was on higher ground, larger, and of a different configuration than the original.

After living in St. Augustine for such a long time, former Mose residents had established themselves there. Some were working at a variety of jobs in town, while others helped forage for food for the townspeople. In spring, some rounded up wild cattle for beef and wild horses for the cavalry. Even so, St. Augustine had a larger population than it could feed. The few food supplies that the Spanish sent from Havana were targets for British corsair raids and were often spoiled if they did reach St. Augustine. The Cuban reinforcements sent earlier had remained in the town, and they and new arrivals from slavery in South Carolina added to the population.

An artist's rendering of the second Fort Mose.

The next governor was interim governor Fulgencio Garcia de Solis. He insisted that the former Mose residents move back to the fort. Many of the former residents felt they were being unfairly evicted. They believed that any truly free people should be able to live wherever they wished. They also knew that the Spanish thought that anyone who lived outside the city walls was less cultivated and somehow inferior to the city dwellers. Residents who had risked their lives fighting in the militia and otherwise contributing to Spanish society considered the interim governor's orders to be an insult. But they could not make him change his mind.

Menendez resumed his leadership positions—as captain of the free militia and chief of the new Mose. The residents built a church and house for the priest, Father Juan Joseph de Solana, inside the fort and twenty-three houses outside the fort for themselves. In 1759, Father Solana conducted a census of the community. This census provided valuable details about the population of Fort Mose. However, it was not possible to know exact ages of adults who had been enslaved and for whom there were no previous records.

Although the residents of Mose had converted to Catholicism, they maintained some of the religious practices that had been meaningful to them in Africa. Like Africans in Cuba, they probably celebrated Catholic feast days wearing African attire and playing African music and instruments. They not only were influenced by the Spanish institutions, but it seems they also influenced the Spanish. An example of this is a pewter medal depicting St. Christopher on one side and a pattern similar to a Kongo star (also called a mariner's compass) on the other.

The Demise of Fort Mose

Francisco Menendez governed the new Mose until 1763, when the Treaty of Paris ended the Anglo-French Seven Years' War. That treaty made Florida a British colony and Cuba a Spanish colony. Mose had always been significant in the disputes between Spain and England. Now, with the signing of a document far across the Atlantic Ocean, Fort Mose and the Spanish presence in St. Augustine came to an end.

The townspeople of St. Augustine, the residents of Mose, and their Indian allies all abandoned their homes and dreams. On August 7, 1763, fifty-one men, women, and children boarded a schooner poignantly named *Nuestra Señora de los Dolores* (Our Lady of Sorrows) and sailed for Cuba. They settled in Matanzas, where they experienced terrible privations. Eventually some, like Francisco Menendez, moved to Havana, further scattering the displaced Mose residents. After living an extraordinary life, Menendez died in Cuba at approximately seventy years of age.

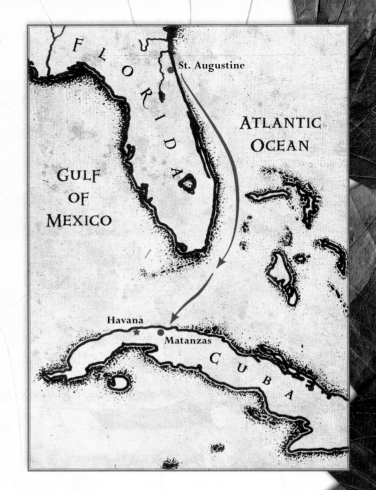

Opposite page: *A description of Fort Mose, written by Father Solana in 1759.*

Above: *A map showing the flight from Florida to Cuba, where many former St. Augustine residents settled.*

The view today of where Fort Mose stood.

AFTERWORD: FORT MOSE TODAY

Although Fort Mose was vacated in 1763—a little more than one hundred years before the end of the American Civil War—the remarkable stories of Francisco Menendez and Fort Mose are still unfolding. They continue to fascinate writers and researchers. Since the 1920s there has been heightened public awareness about the pivotal role Francisco Menendez and Fort Mose played in early American history.

During her travels while collecting folklore in Florida, Zora Neale Hurston found and published information about Fort Mose in a 1927 issue of the *Journal of Negro History*. She gave details from old English documents about the location of Mose and told where a copy of General Oglethorpe's map was available. Several years earlier, journalist Irene Aloha Wright had published her findings about Mose for the same journal.

In 1971 the research of local amateur historian F. E. Williams III convinced him that Fort Mose had been located on land that he owned. He contacted University of Florida archaeologist Charles H. Fairbanks, who conducted test excavations that confirmed the presence of such items as pottery and musket balls. However, those excavations did not find evidence of the fort itself. It was not until 1985, when former state representative Bill Clark and the Black Caucus of the Florida State Legislature secured funding for research into Fort Mose's location, that details of this little-known chapter in American history could be explored.

Archaeologist Dr. Kathleen Deagan of the Florida Museum of Natural History and historian Dr. Jane Landers of Vanderbilt University teamed up. Dr. Landers conducted extensive research on historical documents in Spain and Florida. Her findings guided two years of archaeological digs on F. E. Williams's land. The archaeologists unearthed everyday items that Mose residents used for cooking, shelter, and defense. Prior to that, thermal images of the area had revealed where the first fort was. These images were created by using aircraft-mounted scanners that measure the amount of heat held in the ground in areas where there was human activity. The site of the second fort was found by placing scaled aerial photographs over historic maps to pinpoint the location. A topographical map showed changes in elevation. This suggested where the earthen walls of the new fort once stood. Both Dr. Landers and Dr. Deagan, along with curator Darcie MacMahon, have written extensively on Fort Mose and Francisco Menendez.

Architect Dr. Ralph Johnson of Florida Atlantic University conducted research and interviewed present-day residents of Ceiba Mocha, the black settlement in Cuba where most of the Fort Mose inhabitants relocated after Spain lost Florida. His studies provided new insights into that chapter of their story.

Today nothing of the original Fort Mose can be seen by visitors to the site. After changes in the water level over the years, the land on which it stood is now underwater. The location of the second Fort Mose is on an inaccessible island with no existing structures.

The state of Florida purchased the site of the second fort, and it is now part of the state's park system, two miles north of the Castillo de San Marcos. Visitors can stroll out on a boardwalk, gaze at the island, and imagine what life there was like when Francisco Menendez was the chief. Those who walk from the boardwalk toward the visitors center can read the history of Mose on display boards along the sidewalk. Inside the visitors center, they can see artifacts unearthed by the archaeologists, look at maps and pictures, and gain new historical insights from interactive exhibits. They can imagine life at Mose by reading fictional depictions by such authors as Sharon Draper, James Bullock, and Gertie Laws. Or step into a *chosa* and reflect on what it would have been like to live in one. Each February, visitors can participate in the living-history reenactment Flight to Freedom to get a sense of being one of the townspeople at Mose and knowing Francisco Menendez, the man who achieved the impossible.

Fort Mose has been designated a National Historic Landmark. As the southern end point of the Underground Railroad many years before the birth of the legendary conductor Harriet Tubman, the site is recognized by the National Park Service's Underground Railroad Network to Freedom Program for its significance in providing refuge to those who fled slavery.

AUTHOR'S NOTE

MY GREAT AUNT, BLANCHE SMITH ELLIOTT, HAD AN insatiable curiosity and a lifelong love of learning. These traits were contagious (or is *infectious* a better word?), and her younger family members and students she had taught all "caught" them. Aunt Blanche seemed to know *everything*. Her interests ranged from details of family history to little-known archaeological finds to international developments.

In response, Aunt Blanche's younger sister, Jean Smith Andrews, set herself a secret goal—to one day learn about something before Aunt Blanche did. She achieved her objective when the *New York Times* published a lengthy article about Fort Mose and Francisco Menendez ("Traces of Free Blacks in Florida Uncovered in a Colonial Fort," by Jon Nordheimer, special to the *New York Times*, February 26, 1987, page A14).

When I visited Jean about a week or so later, she greeted me with the news, saying, "I finally found something significant that Blanche didn't know!" Hers and Aunt Blanche's excitement about Fort Mose inspired me to want to learn even more. Finding out that Fort Mose was located just outside St. Augustine, Florida, gave me an additional, personal incentive.

The summer before I entered sixth grade, my father became president of Florida Normal and Industrial Memorial College in St. Augustine, and for the next three years I attended local schools. The fact that no teacher or textbook ever made mention of Fort Mose or Menendez made me especially eager to delve into details of this new discovery. This book is the result.

Since I first learned of Fort Mose, a number of people and circumstances have played a significant role in providing more information. For example, Bettye Smith, an aunt who lives in Florida, sent me an article from her morning paper, which stated that Florida had played a role in the Underground Railroad. The article also mentioned that an Underground Railroad conference would soon be held in Miami. I attended that conference and was able to meet Dr. Jane Landers from Vanderbilt University, who has conducted extensive research into the life of Francisco Menendez and Fort Mose.

Prior to learning of Underground Railroad activity at Fort Mose and elsewhere in Florida, I had had a long-standing interest in the work of Harriet Tubman and the Underground Railroad in the northern United States, where its operations are better known. After publishing *The Underground Railroad in Illinois*, I served on the National Park Service Underground Railroad Advisory Committee, and a National Park Service historian presented a paper about Francisco Menendez and Fort Mose at one of our meetings.

In my continuing study of the subject, I was struck by the story's uniqueness and its relevance to other accounts of enslavement and the quest for freedom. There are many examples. Three that many students are perhaps most familiar with are the poet Phillis Wheatley (who was born and captured in the same African region as Menendez), the *Amistad* incident, and the television miniseries *Roots*.

I hope that learning this previously little-known story will inspire you to "catch" my aunt Blanche's eagerness to find out all you can about subjects that interest you most.

Enjoy your journey.

Acknowledgments

I would like to thank the following people for their contributions to the research for this book. Their interest and expertise have been invaluable.

Since serving on the National Park Service Underground Railroad Advisory Committee for the Underground Railroad Resource Study, I have had ongoing conversations about Fort Mose with Barbara Tagger, program manager of the National Park Service's National Underground Railroad Network to Freedom Program, Southeast Region. She has been most helpful in guiding me to researchers on this and related subjects. Kathleen Bethel, African American studies librarian, Northwestern University Libraries, acquainted me with little-known but most valuable print materials and museum resources.

Professor Joseph Opala of the Department of History at James Madison University, a specialist on the Gullah people and their links to West Africa, has been very generous in sharing insights and information and in responding to questions that arose during the writing of the book. Lois Turner Williams and her son, Lorenzo, provided background on the pioneering research her husband, Dr. Lorenzo Dow Turner, conducted on the Gullah language and its linkage to Sierra Leone. In e-mail correspondence, Harlan Greene of the Addlestone Library of the College of Charleston provided information about early South Carolina documents. Instant messaging made it possible to have online conversations with Queen Quet of the Gullah/Geechee Coalition about specific details of Gullah culture and the technology of rice cultivation.

The research and writings of Dr. Jane Landers of Vanderbilt University, which are based on her extensive research in historic Spanish documents in Spain and Cuba, and Dr. Landers herself, were valuable sources of information about Spanish Florida, St. Augustine, Fort Mose, and Francisco Menendez. Kathryn Davis welcomed and familiarized me with exhibits and interpretive programs at Fort Mose and made the library accessible to me. Hearing Dr. Ralph Johnson speak of his visits to the sites in Cuba where Fort Mose residents had relocated linked the past and the present in a most meaningful way.

Additional thanks to Dr. Michael Gannon, Priscilla Brown, Deborah McKeel, Jenny Masur, Janet Sheard, Bettye Smith, Willie Hart, Jean Andrews, Blanche Elliott, Bobbi Ross, Florida Memorial University, Dr. Barbara Edwards, Gerald Eubanks, David Janes, Al Turner, Wheaton Public Library, Glen Ellyn Public Library, Amistad Research Center, Vivian G. Harsh Collection at the Carter G. Woodson Regional Library of the Chicago Public Library System, Michael Flug, Beverly Cook, Dr. Ralph Johnson, Shirley Wallace, Nelva Hamlin, Dr. Gwen Hankerson, Jackie Perkins, Michael Allen, Fort Lauderdale Public Library, Third World Press, Ann Arcari, Elaine Nichols, Derek Boyd Hankerson, James Bullock, Vera Bunting, Audrey Siler, and Mary Lynne Marquess.

I wish to express special thanks to my publisher, Howard Reeves, for recognizing the importance of making this previously "missing chapter" in American history known; to senior managing editor Scott Auerbach, for his guidance in honing the manuscript; to editorial assistant Brett Wright, for his skill in pairing the illustrations and text; to Maria Middleton, for her design of the book; and to my agent, Scott Mendel, for his support of my work.

Glossary

- **Cacique:** A chief of a community.

- *Chosa*: A hut with a roof of palm fronds.

- **Corsair:** A privateer, or pirate.

- **Middle Passage:** The forced voyage of enslaved Africans across the Atlantic Ocean in squalid conditions lasting weeks and sometimes months.

- **National Historic Landmark:** A historic place of national significance designated by the secretary of the interior because it possesses exceptional value or quality in illustrating or interpreting the heritage of the United States.

- **National Underground Railroad Network to Freedom Program:** The program established by the National Park Service to tell the story of resistance against the institution of slavery in the United States through escape and flight. It came into being as the result of Public Law 105-203, the National Underground Railroad Network to Freedom Act of 1998.

- **Presidio:** A military post in areas under Spanish control.

- **Rice Coast:** A region of West Africa that included the entire area between Senegal and Gambia in the north, and Sierra Leone and Liberia in the south. Africans from this area were sought by South Carolina plantation owners for their agricultural and technical skills in rice cultivation.

- **Seasoning:** The process of breaking the will of enslaved Africans in an effort to make them docile.

- **Thermal image:** An image captured by an infrared camera, which measures temperature variations and reveals sites that radiate different concentrations of heat. Archaeologists use thermal images to measure the amount of heat held in ground areas (even those that are underwater) that were occupied or altered by farming or structures. Thermal images also have many applications in medicine, the military, and industry.

NOTES

Works cited are listed in full in Sources.

Page 3: "The state of affairs among these people . . . anything to fear from robbers or men of violence." W. E. B. Du Bois, *The World and Africa*, p. 209.

Page 5: "The filth, the stench, the loss of life . . . the journey known as the Middle Passage or Maafa ('the massive disaster')." Velma Maia Thomas, *Lest We Forget: The Passage from Africa to Slavery and Emancipation*, p. 6.

Page 11: "while most of the hunting and trapping was done by Indians . . . returned downstream with boatloads of skins." Peter H. Wood, *Black Majority: Negroes in Colonial South Carolina from 1670 Through the Stono Rebellion*, pp. 114–15.

Page 13: "In simple proportional terms . . . never been adequately pieced together," "dismal in all respects . . . Lives are Threatened," and "Their importance was increased . . . aid from Virginia." Ibid., pp. 125–26.

Page 13: "[A]ll we can doe is . . . Judgement upon us." Edward Ball, *Slaves in the Family*, p. 95.

Page 14: "liberty to all . . . the men as well as the women . . ." Jane Landers, *Fort Mose: Gracia Real de Santa Teresa de Mose: A Free Black Town in Spanish Colonial Florida*, p. 11.

Page 18: "more than loyal" and "heathen." Ibid., p. 13.

Page 18: "good customs." Ibid., p. 16.

Page 20: "fortress of freedom." Kathleen Deagan and Darcie MacMahon. *Fort Mose: Colonial America's Black Fortress of Freedom*, p. vii.

Page 20: "four square with a flanker at each corner . . . and a lookout" and "running through it." Ibid., p. 15.

Page 21: "resembling thatched Indian huts." Ibid., p. 15.

Page 21: "the most cruel enemies of the English" and "their last drop of blood . . . the Holy Faith." Ibid., p. 16.

Page 24: "for he was . . . kind to his slaves." Wood, *Black Majority*, p. 315.

Page 27: "distinguished himself in the establishment and cultivation of Mose . . . would apply themselves to work and learn good customs." Ibid., pp. 19–20.

Page 27: "loyalty, zeal, and love . . . especially on this occasion." Ibid., p. 20.

Page 28: "pickled him." Ibid., p. 23.

Sources

Books and Periodicals

Ball, Edward. *Slaves in the Family*. New York: Farrar, Straus and Giroux, 1998.

Berlin, Ira. *Many Thousands Gone*. Cambridge, Mass., and London, England: The Belknap Press of Harvard University Press, 1998.

Colburn, David, and Jane Landers, eds. "Traditions of African American Freedom and Community in Spanish Florida." *The African American Heritage of Florida*. Gainesville: University Press of Florida, 1995.

Curtin, Philip. *Economic Change in Precolonial Africa: Senegambia in the Era of the Slave Trade*. Madison: University of Wisconsin Press, 1975.

Davidson, Basil, and the editors of Time-Life Books. *African Kingdoms*. New York: Time-Life Books, 1971.

Deagan, Kathleen, and Darcie MacMahon. *Fort Mose: Colonial America's Black Fortress of Freedom*. Gainesville: University Press of Florida, 1995.

DeWolf, Thomas Norman. *Inheriting the Trade: A Northern Family Confronts Its Legacy as the Largest Slave-Trading Dynasty in U.S. History*. Boston: Beacon Press, 2008.

Du Bois, W. E. B. *The World and Africa*. New York: International Publishers, 1947.

Gates, Henry Louis, Jr., ed. *The Classic Slave Narratives*. New York: Mentor, 1987.

Goodwine, Marquetta L. *Gullah/Geechee: Africa's Seeds in the Winds of the Diaspora*. Vol. 5. Beaufort, S.C.: Kinship Publications, 2006.

Hansen, Joyce, and Gary McGowan. *Freedom Roads: Searching for the Underground Railroad*. Chicago: Cricket Books, 2003.

Jackson, John G. *Introduction to African Civilizations*. New York: University Books, 1970.

Landers, Jane. *Black Society in Spanish Florida*. Urbana: University of Illinois Press, 1999.

————. *Fort Mose: Gracia Real de Santa Teresa de Mose: A Free Black Town in Spanish Colonial Florida*. St. Augustine, Fla.: St. Augustine Historical Society, 1992. (Reprinted from *American Historical Review* 95, no. 1 [Fall 1990].)

————. "Slavery in the Lower South." *OAH Magazine of American History* 17, no. 3 (April 2003): 23–27.

————. "Southern Passage: The Forgotten Route to Freedom." In *Passages to Freedom: The Underground Railroad in American History and Memory*, ed. David Blight. Washington, D.C.: Smithsonian Institution Press, 2004.

Landers, Jane G., ed. *Against the Odds: Free Blacks in the Slave Societies of the Americas*. London: Frank Cass & Co. Ltd, 1996.

Landers, Jane G., with Kathleen A. Deagan. "Fort Mose: Earliest Free African-American Town in the United States." In *"I, Too, Am America": Archaeological Studies of African-American Life*, ed. Theresa A. Singleton. Charlottesville: University of Virginia Press, 1999.

Leacock, Elspeth, and Susan Buckley. *Places in Time: A New Atlas of American History*. Boston: Houghton Mifflin, 2001.

Rodney, Walter. *A History of the Upper Guinea Coast, 1545–1800*. Oxford: Clarendon Press, 1970.

Schaffer, Matt, and Christine Cooper. *Mandinko: The Ethnography of a West African Holy Land*. Prospect Heights, Ill.: Waveland Press, 1987.

Thomas, Velma Maia. *Lest We Forget: The Passage from Africa to Slavery and Emancipation*. New York: Crown, 1997.

Thompson, Kathleen, and Hilary Mac Austin, eds. *The Face of Our Past: Images of Black Women from Colonial America to the Present*. Bloomington: Indiana University Press, 1999.

Turner, Lorenzo D. *Africanisms in the Gullah Dialect*. Columbia: University Press of South Carolina, 1949 [2002].

Wood, Peter H. *Black Majority: Negroes in Colonial South Carolina from 1670 Through the Stono Rebellion*. New York: Alfred A. Knopf, Inc., 1974.

Internet Resources

African History
www.buzzle.com/articles/history-of-mandingo-tribe.html
www.cocc.edu/cagatucci/classes/hum211/timelines/htimelinetoc.htm
library.stanford.edu/depts/ssrg/africa/guide.html
www.metmuseum.org/toah/hd/mali/hd_mali.htm

Gullah/Geechee Sea Island Culture
www.officialgullahgeechee.info
www.yale.edu/glc/gullah/index.htm

St. Augustine and Fort Mose
www.flmnh.ufl.edu/staugustine/intro.htm
www.floridastateparks.org/fortmose
www.fortmose.com
www.fortmose.org
www.scenica1a.org/Fort_Mose.aspx

Transatlantic Slave Trade
www.liverpoolmuseums.org.uk/ism

Underground Railroad
www.cr.nps.gov/ugrr
www.npca.org/cultural_diversity/black_history/ugrr.html

ILLUSTRATION CREDITS

Opposite title page: Florida Museum of Natural History (drawing by Bill Celander); opposite page 1: The Lionel Pincus and Princess Firyal Map Division, The New York Public Library, Astor, Lenox & Tilden Foundations; page 1: Courtesy Project Gutenberg; page 2: General Research Division, The New York Public Library, Astor, Lenox & Tilden Foundations; page 3 (left): Bibliotheque National de France; page 3 (right): Franko Khoury, National Museum of African Art, Smithsonian Institution; page 4 (top): National Maritime Museum, Greenwich, UK; page 4 (center): Barry Williams; page 5: Manuscripts, Archives and Rare Books Division, Schomburg Center for Research in Black Culture, The New York Public Library, Astor, Lenox & Tilden Foundations; page 6: Print Collection, Miriam and Ira D. Wallach Division of Art, Prints and Photographs, The New York Public Library, Astor, Lenox & Tilden Foundations; page 7 (top): Picture Collection, The New York Public Library, Astor, Lenox & Tilden Foundations; page 7 (bottom left): The South Carolina Historical Society; page 7 (bottom right): American Antiquarian Society; page 8: Robert N. Dennis Collection of Stereoscopic Views, Miriam and Ira D. Wallach Division of Art, Prints and Photographs, The New York Public Library, Astor, Lenox & Tilden Foundations; page 9: Robert N. Dennis Collection of Stereoscopic Views, Miriam and Ira D. Wallach Division of Art, Prints and Photographs, The New York Public Library, Astor, Lenox & Tilden Foundations; page 10: Abby Aldrich Rockefeller Folk Art Museum, The Colonial Williamsburg Foundation, Williamsburg, VA; page 12: Florida Museum of Natural History—Historical Archaeology Collection; page 14: www.history-map.com; page 15: Historical Museum of Southern Florida; page 16: Library of Congress; page 17 (top): Joseph Hefter, *Artes de Mexico,* No. 102, 1968; page 17 (bottom): Original sources unknown, appears in *Historia de España, vol. 5,* Ferran Soldevila (Barcelona, Ariel, 1964); page 19 (top): Reprinted from *The Houses of St. Augustine,* Albert Manusy (St. Augustine Historical Society, 1978); page 19 (bottom left): Pedro Ruiz de Olano, 1738; P.K. Yonge Library of Florida History, Gainesville; page 19 (bottom right): James Moncrief, 1765; page 20: Library of Congress; page 21: Theodore deBry, *America* (Frankfurt, 1596); page 22 (left and right): Print Collection, Miriam and Ira D. Wallach Division of Art, Prints and Photographs, The New York Public Library, Astor, Lenox & Tilden Foundations; page 23 (left): Joachim Monteiro, *Angola and the River Congo* (London: Macmillan, 1875); page 23 (right): Library of Congress; page 24: Picture Collection, The New York Public Library, Astor, Lenox & Tilden Foundations; page 25: Library of Congress; page 26: Emmet Collection, Miriam and Ira D. Wallach Division of Art, Prints and Photographs, The New York Public Library, Astor, Lenox & Tilden Foundations; page 29: Florida Museum of Natural History—Historical Archaeology Collection; page 30: Courtesy P.K. Yonge Library of Florida History, Gainesville; page 31: Adapted from *Fort Mose: Colonial America's Black Fortress of Freedom*, University Press of Florida, Florida Museum of Natural History; page 32: Courtesy Glennette Tilley Turner.

INDEX

Page numbers in italics refer to illustrations.